2021

Coloring
Calendar
UNICORNS & RAINBOWS

2021

Sun.	Mon.	Tue.	Wed.	Thu.	Fri.	Sat.
					1 New Year's Day	2
3	4	5	6	7	8	9
10	11	12	13	14	15	16
17	18 Martin Luther King, Jr. Day	19	20	21	22	23
24	25	26	27	28	29	30
31						

2021

Sun.	Mon.	Tue.	Wed.	Thu.	Fri.	Sat.
	1	2	3	4	5	6
7	8	9	10	11	12	13
14 Valentine's Day	15 Presidents' Day	16	17	18	19	20
21	22	23	24	25	26	27
28						

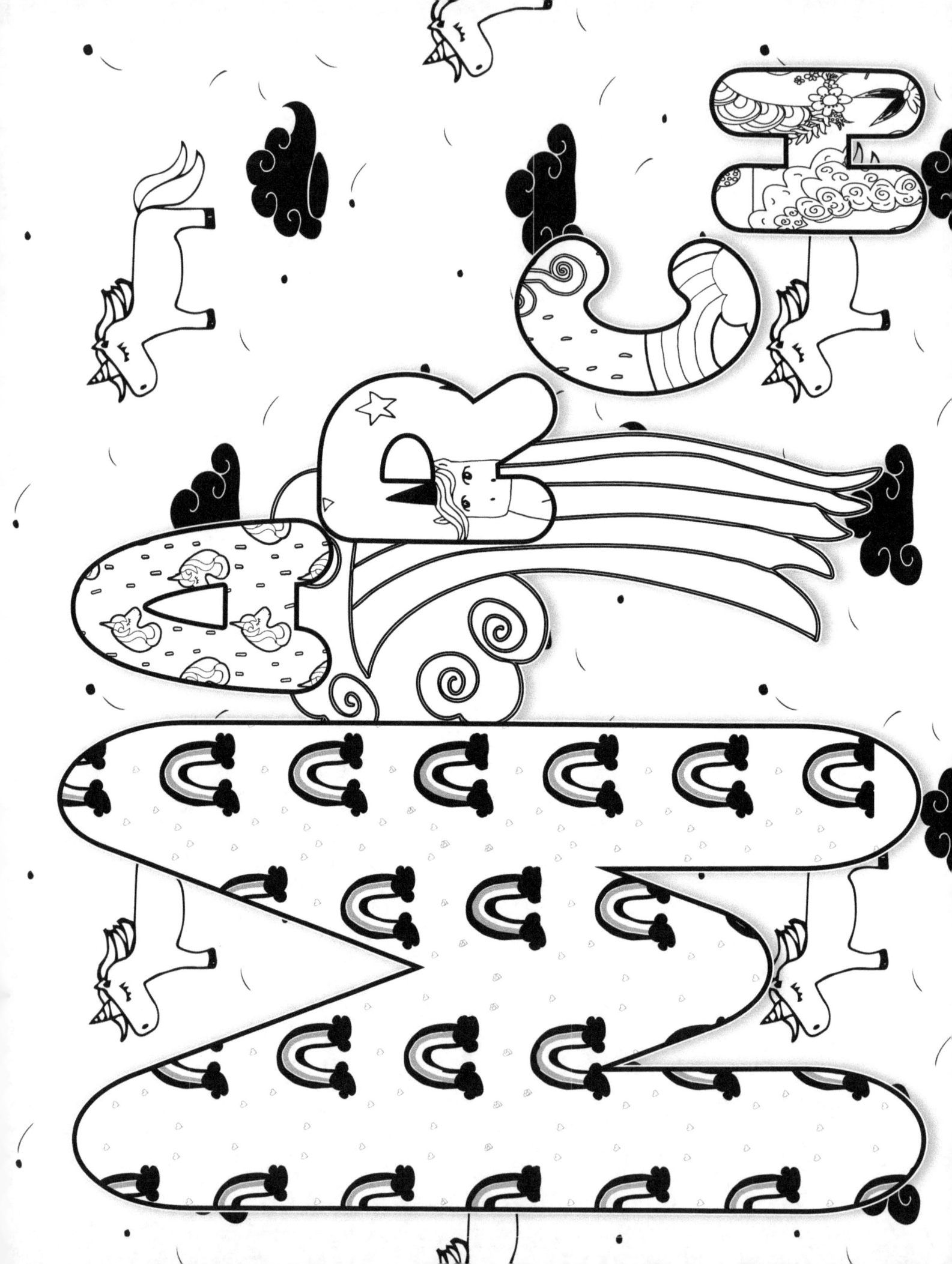

2021

Sun.	Mon.	Tue.	Wed.	Thu.	Fri.	Sat.
	1	2	3	4	5	6
7	8	9	10	11	12	13
14 Daylight Saving Time Begins	15	16	17 St. Patrick's Day	18	19	20
21	22	23	24	25	26	27
28	29	30	31			

2021

Sun.	Mon.	Tue.	Wed.	Thu.	Fri.	Sat.
				1	2	3
4 Easter	5	6	7	8	9	10
11	12	13	14	15	16	17
18	19	20	21	22	23	24
25	26	27	28	29	30	

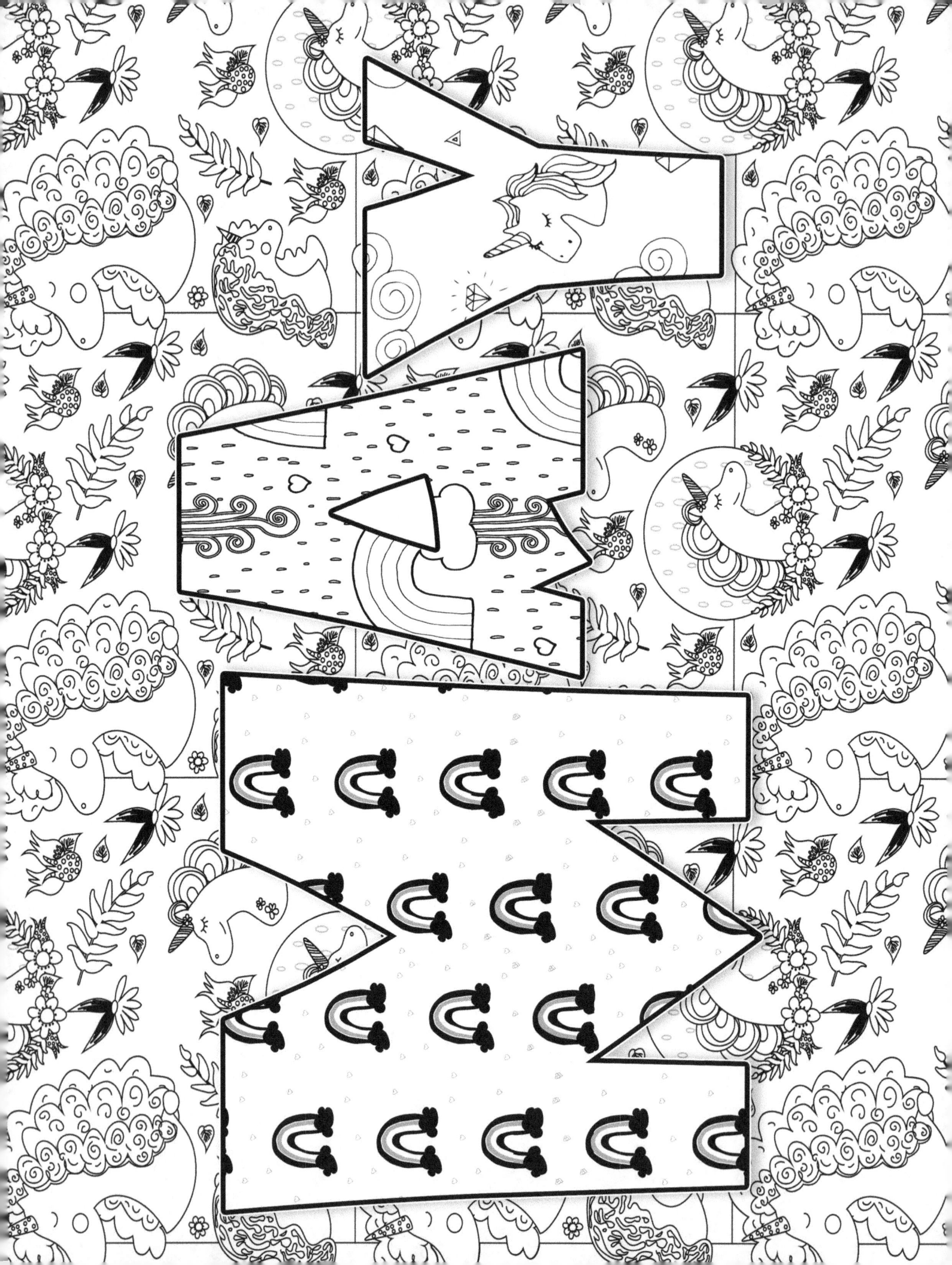

2021

Sun.	Mon.	Tue.	Wed.	Thu.	Fri.	Sat.
						1
2	3	4	5	6	7	8
9 Mother's Day	10	11	12	13	14	15
16	17	18	19	20	21	22
23	24	25	26	27	28	29
30	31 Memorial Day					

2021

Sun.	Mon.	Tue.	Wed.	Thu.	Fri.	Sat.
		1	2	3	4	5
6	7	8	9	10	11	12
13	14	15	16	17	18	19
20 Father's Day	21	22	23	24	25	26
27	28	29	30			

2021

Sun.	Mon.	Tue.	Wed.	Thu.	Fri.	Sat.
				1	2	3
4 Independence Day	5 Independence Day Observed	6	7	8	9	10
11	12	13	14	15	16	17
18	19	20	21	22	23	24
25	26	27	28	29	30	31

2021

Sun.	Mon.	Tue.	Wed.	Thu.	Fri.	Sat.
1	2	3	4	5	6	7
8	9	10	11	12	13	14
15	16	17	18	19	20	21
22	23	24	25	26	27	28
29	30	31				

2021

Sun.	Mon.	Tue.	Wed.	Thu.	Fri.	Sat.
			1	2	3	4
5	6 Labor Day	7	8	9	10	11
12	13	14	15	16	17	18
19	20	21	22	23	24	25
26	27	28	29	30		

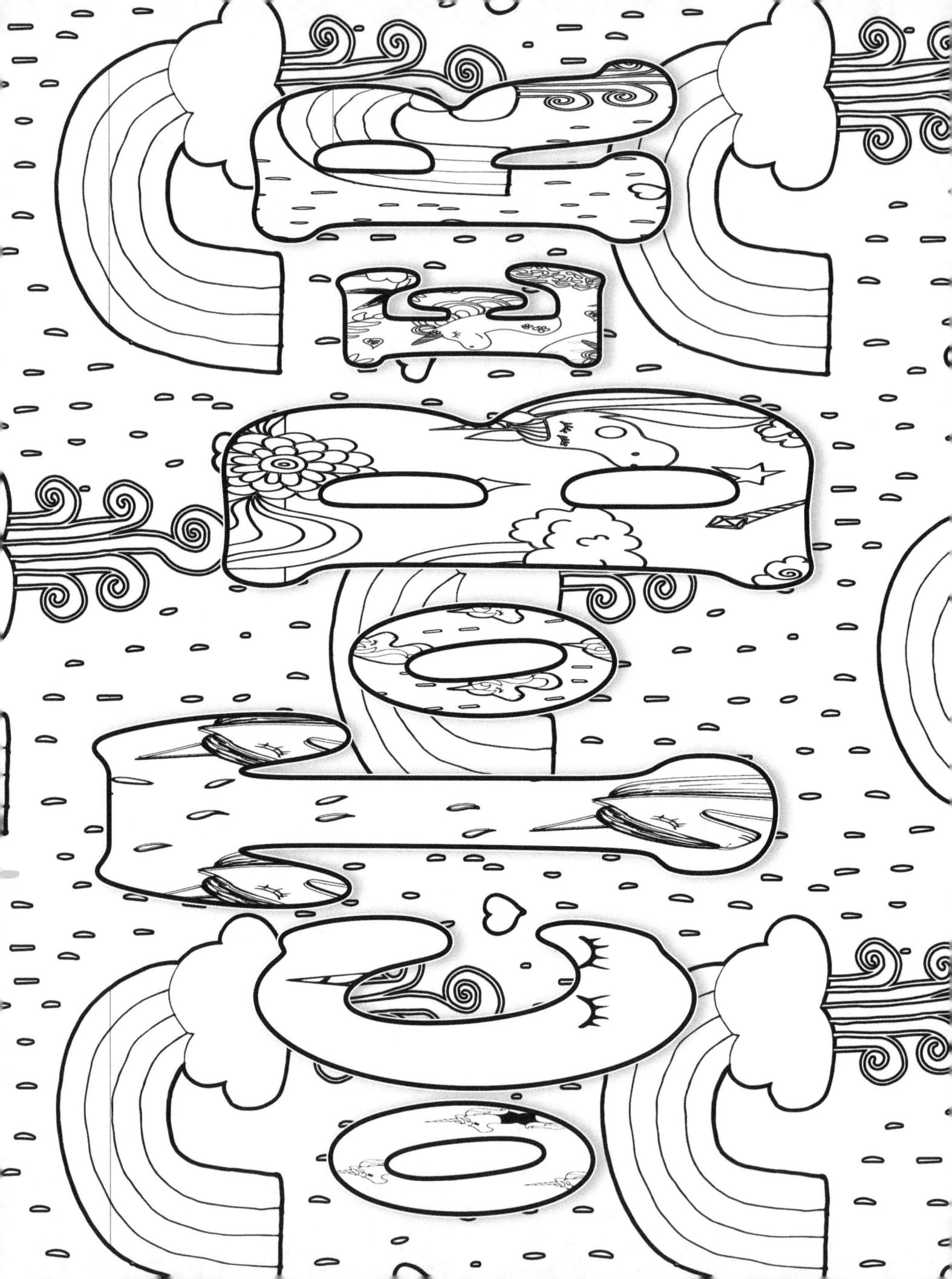

2021

Sun.	Mon.	Tue.	Wed.	Thu.	Fri.	Sat.
					1	2
3	4	5	6	7	8	9
10	11 Columbus Day	12	13	14	15	16
17	18	19	20	21	22	23
24	25	26	27	28	29	30
31 Halloween						

2021

Sun.	Mon.	Tue.	Wed.	Thu.	Fri.	Sat.
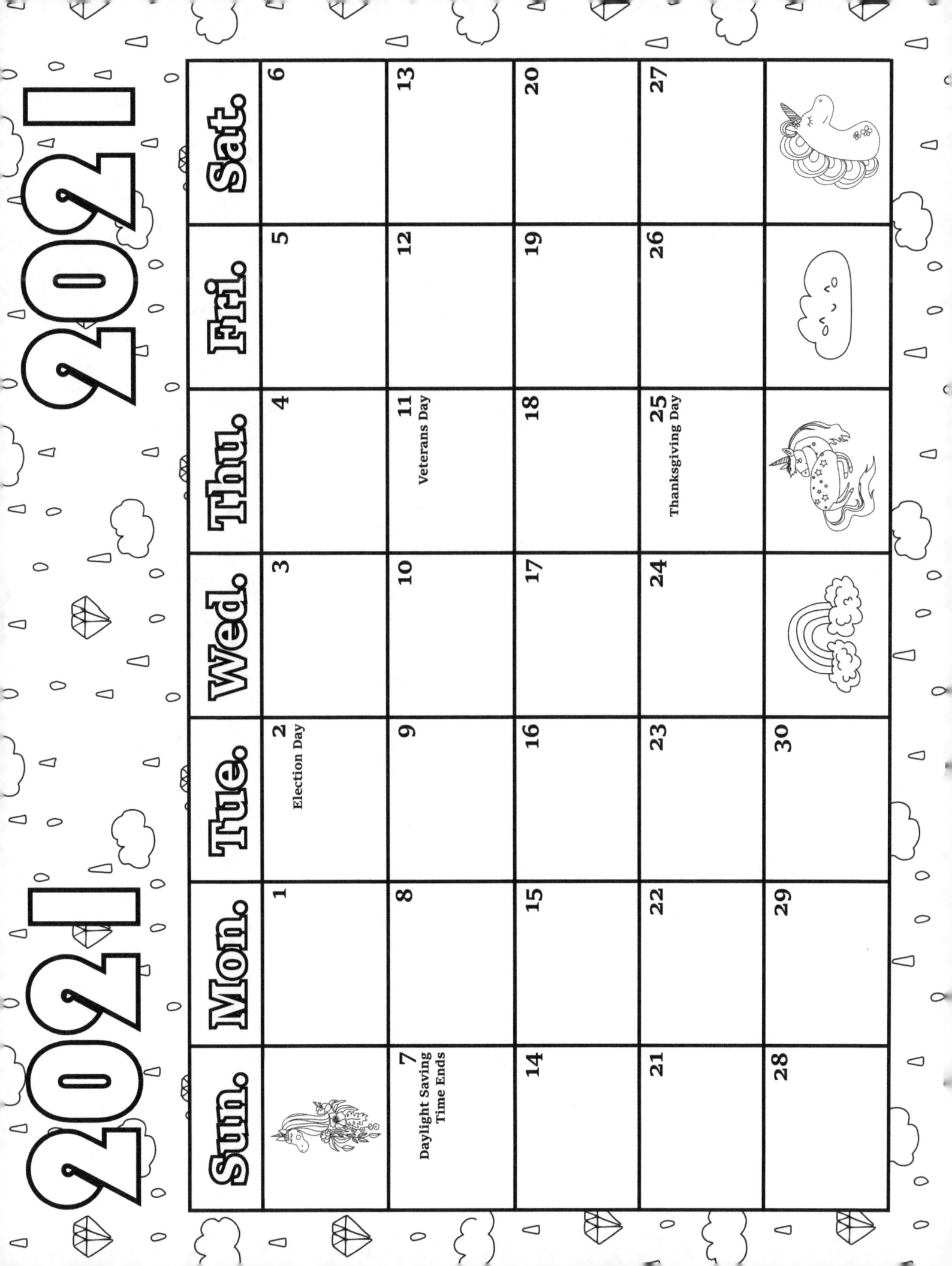	1	2 Election Day	3	4	5	6
7 Daylight Saving Time Ends	8	9	10	11 Veterans Day	12	13
14	15	16	17	18	19	20
21	22	23	24	25 Thanksgiving Day	26	27
28	29	30				

2021

Sun.	Mon.	Tue.	Wed.	Thu.	Fri.	Sat.
			1	2	3	4
5	6	7	8	9	10	11
12	13	14	15	16	17	18
19	20	21	22	23	24 **Christmas Observed**	25 **Christmas**
26	27	28	29	30	31 **New Year's Day Observed**